A Parent's Book For Children

The Adventures Of
TEAM LITTLE BIGS

Created by Jonathan T. Gilliam
Illustrated by Danielle Kriner

Post Hill
PRESS

A POST HILL PRESS BOOK
ISBN: 978-1-64293-577-6

The Adventures of Team Little Bigs:
A Parent's Book for Children
© 2020 by Jonathan T. Gilliam
All Rights Reserved

Cover and interior art by Danielle Kriner

Post Hill Press
New York • Nashville
posthillpress.com

Published in the United States of America

Dedicated to each and every soul that God chooses to send into this world. May this book be a foundation for your safety and awareness so you may live long, fruitful lives.

In remembrance of all the animals that touch our lives and make us better people. May the impact of this book reflect the impact you have in our lives.

May the blessing of God be upon this book and the example of his son Jesus reflected within its teachings.

The Adventures of TEAM LITTLE BIGS: A Parent's Book for Children was created by Jonathan T. Gilliam, a former US Navy SEAL and FBI Special Agent, and artistic illustrator, Danielle Kriner. Through this unique collaboration of security expertise and artistic creativity, Gilliam and Kriner have created a children's book that helps parents emphasize communication in situations that can be completely predicted and avoided.

TEAM LITTLE BIGS characters bring an emotional and expressive interactive experience, reflecting the intelligent, curious, and loving personalities of Gilliam's dogs—Rico, Jesse, and Bonnie Sue—and the feisty personality of Meow Meow, who represents every cat that has ever lived. The downloadable lesson plans are available for free at www.TeamLittleBigs.com, where parents sign up and use the specifically crafted lesson plans with the book's respective pictures. These lesson plans will guide parents as their children flip through each picture, ensuring that the specific lessons vital to safety and awareness are clearly communicated.

Each lesson plan was created by a collaborative effort between Gilliam and educational expert Tracey Alvino, with critical review and input from psychologist Dr. Laura Bartels, Psy.D. Every detail of the lesson plans has been considered and placed online, separate from the book, so parents can seamlessly point out the specifics of each pictured situation, as their children get uninterrupted time with the characters. This structured interaction will help children identify situations they need to avoid and remind parents where potential issues exist, culminating in the development of advanced understanding and communication abilities.

The Adventures of TEAM LITTLE BIGS is truly a parent's book that can be used to keep children safer, a.k.a. "A Parent's Book for Children."

Rico

Meow Meow

Jesse

Bonnie Sue

THE BIGS FAMILY INFORMATION

Mom: Mary Bigs

Dad: George Bigs

Kids: Rico, Jesse, Bonnie Sue,
Meow Meow

Address:
2356 Freedom Place
Beautiful Sky, AZ, 12345

Phone Number:
555-555-1234

31

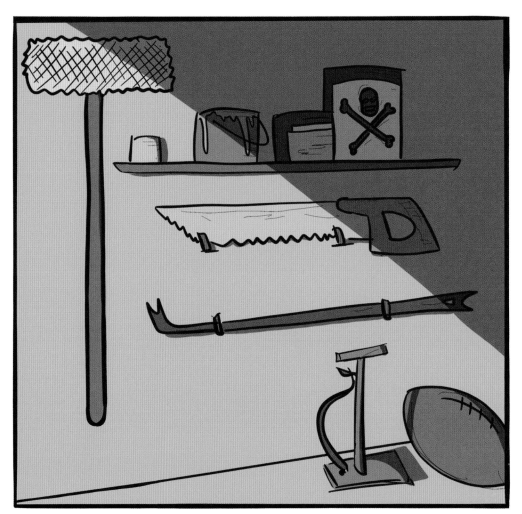

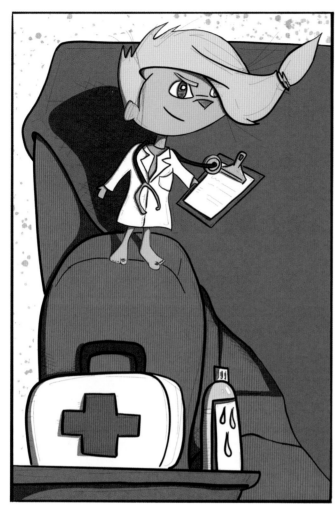

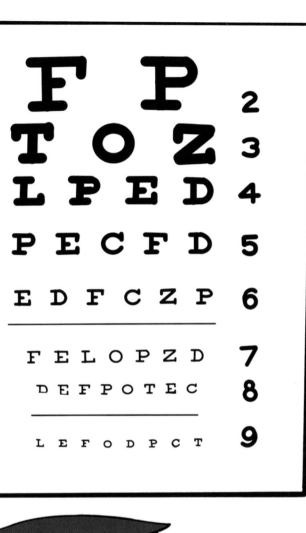

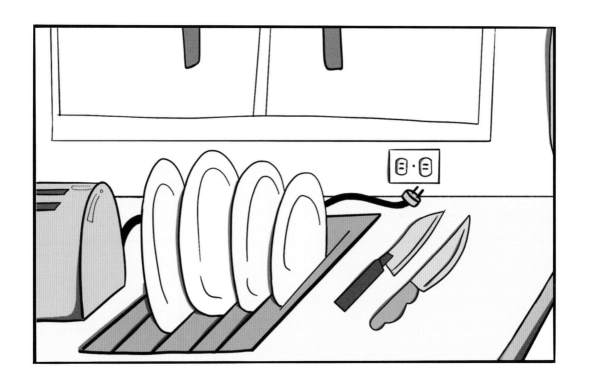

BEDTIME ROUTINE

- Go potty
- Take a bath
- Wash everywhere!
- Brush teeth
- Brush each tooth
- Put on pajamas
- Say goodnight to everyone Dog, Mom, Dad, Sister, Brother
- Say your prayers
- Drink water
- Bedtime story

THE

END

JONATHAN T. GILLIAM is a career public servant with over twenty years of service as a Navy SEAL, FBI Special Agent, Federal Air Marshal, Private Security Contractor, Police Officer, Public Speaker, and Expert Media Commentator. Gilliam has extensive experience in crisis management, threat analysis and mitigation, small unit leadership, on-scene command, and special events crisis management. Gilliam has a BA in Psychology (emphasis in Developmental Psychology) and Political Science (emphasis on the Executive Branch) and he is the author of the bestselling book Sheep No More: The Art of Awareness and Attack Survival.

DANIELLE KRINER is an oil painter and illustrator specializing in portraits. She has twenty-two years of quality experience in the brewing industry and is a NASM certified personal trainer. Kriner studied biology and holds a BA in Art from York College of Pennsylvania.